by Frances Gilbert
illustrated by Eren Unten

Random House New York

It is time
to get ready
for school.
I put on my dress.

I put on my socks.

I put on my shoes.

I put on my tutu!

"No, you can not
wear a tutu
to school."

"But I love my tutu!"

It is time to get ready
for swimming lessons.
I put on my swimsuit.
I put on my swim cap.
I put on my swim goggles.

I put on my tutu!

“No, you can not
wear a tutu
for swimming lessons.”

“But I love my tutu!”

It is time to get ready for soccer.
I put on my uniform.

I put on my shin guards.

I put on my cleats.

I put on my tutu!

“No, you can not wear a tutu for soccer.”

“But I love my tutu!”

“Can I wear my tutu to art class?”

“No, you can not
wear a tutu
to art class.”

“Can I wear my tutu camping?”

“No, you can not wear a tutu camping!”

"Can I wear my tutu to the fair?"

Roller Coaster

“No, you can not
wear a tutu
to the fair.”

“BUT I LOVE MY TUTU!”

"Can I wear my tutu to ballet class?"

"Yes! You <u>can</u>
wear your tutu
to ballet class!"

# “I LOVE MY TUTU!”

"We love our tutus, too!"